Once upon a time, there lived two families in a community called Kabaray. They were living together peacefully till they were struck by famine. That exposed their true colors. They totally depended on subsistence farming, but there was an outbreak of pests in their community that destroyed all their crops. It was very tough for them to endure hence, the family heads by the names of Mr. Bankoloh and Mr. Yikiban came together to find a means to sustain their families. Following a lengthy discussion, they agreed to go out and seek assistance from one of their neighboring communities. They agreed to take-off the following day. They all discussed it with their family members, and they were all excited about the move their breadwinners planned to make. They went to bed on tenterhooks for success in the next two days.

At around 6:00 am, Mr. Bankoloh woke up and went to Mr. Yikiban's residence, calling for him to get geared up. *"Mr. Yikiban, Are you ready for the jungle? yes, I am ready!"* replied Mr. Yikiban joyously. They got prepared and took off. Mr. Bankoloh and his companion went through the journey as a team peacefully; they neither quarreled nor disagreed. On their way to the farms of their neighboring community, they met a knoll, so both of them decided to rest for a while at that place. They were also able to sight the farms from that point, but it was too far for them to know the fate of their trip. While they were sleeping, Mr. Bankoloh began planning how to get the larger share because he saw himself as smarter than his friend. His aim was for him to get more rice (which was the staple food in that region) than Mr. Yikiban. He sat down quietly, planning and looking at the condition of the farms from afar, judging in his mind that only the farm where the smoke was imminent seemed to be good and fruitful. After his speculations, he made up a decision in his mind, saying *"Oh yes! That's it. I will indirectly force him to continue his journey to the farm where there is no smoke, because there are fewer chances there for success. We will no longer work as a squad."* After they rested for a while, Mr. Bankoloh stood up and told Mr. Yikiban that they were no more a team. He told his friend that they both have to try very hard to get what each of them deserves. He held Mr. Yikiban's hand, saying, *"You see that farm"* (pointing at the farm house with no smoke)? *Everything you get from that farm is yours; don't count me in. I will strike on my own and don't expect anything from me. I will go to the farm over there (pointing at the farm house that has a lot of smoke coming out of its hut)."* Mr. Yikiban disagreed with his decision, preferring that they work as a team and share whatever they achieve as brothers from the same community. He looked at Mr. Bankoloh, and he wanted to comment on his decision, but Mr. Bankoloh never gave him the opportunity to do so.

Mr. Bankoloh left while his friend (Mr. Yikiban) was still standing there contemplating what his friend had said from the beginning of the journey to the present pronouncement he made. He prayed for God to support and direct him through the jungle. He breathed deeply and said, *"Oh my God! What kind of thing is this? Anyway, Papa God see me through"* and then he took off towards the destination projected to him by Mr. Bankoloh.

He arrived at the farm, and luckily he met them harvesting. Surprisingly to him, he was welcomed as if he was one of their family members. He introduced himself and explained his sticky situation to them. They all felt pity for him, and they gave him food without delay. *Oh my dear! You are blessed. You can harvest any amount you are able to carry. "Feel free to ask any question. We are now going to carry on the harvesting,"* says the family head by the name of Mr. Gbahoi. *"OK sir, thank you very much for coming to my aid,"* replied Mr. Yikiban. After he had finished eating and rested a bit, he joined them in harvesting.

The members of the Gbahoi family were all in high spirits for the chance God gave them to rescue someone like him, because they believed in helping people, especially those with pressing needs. The Gbahoi family encouraged Mr. Yikiban to have courage, and they all agreed to help him with any amount of rice he is able to carry. In the early hours of the sundown, Mr. Yikiban, with the help of Mr. Gbahoi's children, threshed four (4) bushels of rice, but he measured only two (2) bushels, which he believed he was able to carry without help. Mr. Gbahoi promised Mr. Yikiban that he would always keep him in mind and be ready to help him whenever he was in need.

On the other hand, Mr. Bankoloh was moving gleefully towards the farm he chose, but his happiness died out without a notice.

As he approached the farm, he noticed that there was no sign of ready-for-harvest rice in the field. The rice was in its milky stage, so his hope for success vanished. In place of entering the farm, he said, *"Oh my God! What's the hell I'm getting myself into? Anyway, let me reach out and see what is going on"*. He approached the farm house wretchedly.

When he arrived at the house, he knocked and entered, pretending to be happy. After he had exercised their customary way of greeting, he started explaining his problem and the reason for his visit. By the time he ended his elucidation, the family head by the name of Mr. Kuwayn interrupted, clearly telling him that success was not in his favor. He told Mr. Bankoloh that they too were now short of their principal food (which is rice). *"I'm sorry, Mr. Bankoloh; we should have assisted you, but we don't have the resources right now. Corn and bush yams are now the only foods available for our survival,"* says Mr. Kuwayn. He took some bush yam and corn and gave them to Mr. Bankoloh, but he was unable to eat them because his expectations were completely ruined. He was sitting there wordless for over an hour.

He later made up his mind to go and perceive what was going on in the farm where he had circuitously forced Mr. Yikiban to go. On his way to the farm, he stingily ate the corn and yams Mr. Kuwayn gave him, thinking that Mr. Yikiban was in an identical situation.

As he approached the farm house of Mr. Gbahoi, he saw Mr. Yikiban and Mr. Gbahoi sitting down discussing and making fun.

When he saw the harvested rice of Mr. Gbahoi, he regretfully shook his head. He regretted his actions towards Mr. Yikiban, but he felt too proud to apologize.

As he arrived Mr. Bankoloh exercised his traditional rite as a stranger (that is, greeting); Mr. Yikiban introduced him to the Gbahoi family as his best friends from the same community.

Mr. Yikiban took his friend into his temporary hut, which has two (2) opposite beds. It was one of the best huts in the farm, which the Gbahoi family uses as temporary accommodation for strangers.

Mr. Yikiban wanted to help him, but Mr. Bankoloh's response totally destroyed his desire to help him. Mr. Yikiban showed him his two (2) bushels of rice.

"My brother what about you? Have you succeeded?" asked Mr. Yikiban. Mr. Bankoloh replied, *"I'm OK my friend! Whether I succeed or not, it's none of your business! My family and I will make it up."* He stood still, reflecting on Mr. Bankoloh's response and his preceding behavior towards him. Finally, he decided not to help him anymore. *"Ok bro, I just wanted to help you."* Mr. Bankoloh replied again harshly, *"Hey my man! Without your help, my family and I will still survive"*. Mr. Yikiban treated his reactions politely, and together they went out wordless, pretending as if everything was OK. He had leftover rice, but just because his friend was not polite with him, he decided not to give it to him.

It was time for them to go to siesta; Mr. Yikiban noticed that his friend may have stolen his leftover cooked rice overnight. So he made up his mind to scam him by secretly tying cowries on his eyebrows.

While they were in their room, Mr. Yikiban timed his friend for him to secretly tie the cowries on his eyebrows. When Mr. Bankoloh went out to ease himself, he quickly tied the cowries on his eyebrows and went to bed.

Later Mr. Bankoloh came in and sat on the bed opposite to the one where Mr. Yikiban was lying; at that time and he was already sleeping. Mr. Bankoloh thought that his friend was still wide awake because he saw the cowries shining on his face, thinking that it were his eyes shining. He thought that Mr. Yikiban was monitoring him (not asleep) for his leftover rice. He said, *"My friend, you will not sleep today. You think that I will eat your rice? Uh!"* He spent the whole night sleepless, monitoring his friend, but Mr. Yikiban was busy sleeping.

When it was dawn, Mr. Yikiban woke up and secretly removed the cowries. When they were ready to return home, Mr. Yikiban did not want to officially tell his friend to help him carry the rice, as it could be a potential means for Mr. Bankoloh to ask for a share of the rice. So he tied the rice in one bag, planning to trick him again. They gave leave-taking to the Gbahoi family and took off.

As soon as they left, they were no longer talking to each other. Since Mr. Yikiban never made an attempt to help him, he decided to test him to see if he would decide to help him or steal the rice. He placed the rice on the side of the road and went into the bush, pretending to be pressed by nature.

Mr. Bankoloh took the rice when he affirmed that his friend was out of site and started running away with it. Mr. Yikiban came out, and he did not see the rice. He was contemplating whether Mr. Bankoloh was trying to steal his rice or trying to help him. Hence, he planned to go ahead of him using shortcut roads talking to himself: *"I will teach him a lesson if he tries to steal my rice."* He ran through the bush in such a way that Mr. Bankoloh didn't set eyes on him. He went ahead of him and lied down on the roadside. He disguised as if it was his children lying down on the road helplessly waiting for him to come back home. When Mr. Bankoloh met him, he thought that it was Mr. Yikiban's children. He said, *"Hmmm... you are coming after your dad.*

You think that he got something, but he didn't get a seed." Mr. Yikiban acted the same way repeatedly, and Mr. Bankoloh repeated the same statement. He finally understood that Mr. Bankoloh was not trying to help him but rather stealing his rice.

When he met Mr. Yikiban at the third location, he said, *"Oh! I have traps here. Let me quickly check them."* Mr. Yikiban said in his mind (where he was lying down): *"That's good. Now it is my town." I will teach this devil a lesson."* As he was going into the bush to check his traps, Mr. Yikiban stood up and replaced the rice with sand. He carried the rice home and saved his family from starving to death. Mr. Bankoloh came back from the bush empty handed and quickly collected the load and carried it home, not knowing it was sand.

When his wife and children saw him coming, sweating, not knowing he was carrying sand, they started singing and dancing. They kept on singing, *"Kuyain ko thu kanu satuku." Kuyain ko thu kanu satuku. Kuyain ko thu kanu satuku. Kuyain ko thu kanu satuku."* This is a Limba song, which means that a tree that God has planted will never die.

From this perspective, it indirectly means that as long as it is God that created them, they will never die of hunger. His wife was so happy that she didn't even know what to do next. She called her husband in their room and asked him, *"How is the journey? How about your friend, how many bags has he got? Eh Bags? He's got nothing."* Mr. Bankoloh replied. His wife was astonished by her husband's statement and said in her heart: *"Hmm... something is wrong.*

How can that be possible? I believe that they went out as a team. He must have done something to that poor man.” After a while, she responded to her husband's statement by saying, *"If he got nothing, how are they going to survive? That is not my concern. What is important is that I have got something for my family. "Please bring me a bucket of water to the wash yard,"* replied Mr. Bankoloh.

Mrs. Bankoloh fetched the water from the well and took it to the wash yard. She was not happy with her husband's statement, but she had nothing to do. The reason is that their tradition did not permit women to make opposing statements or decisions to their husbands. She was quiet while she waits for her husband to finish taking a bath and hand over the rice to her for further processing.

After Mr. Bankoloh had finished refreshing himself, he handed over the rice to his wife, saying, *"Take care of the rice and make sure that you manage it well. I will,"* replied Mrs. Bankoloh. She took a bowl and went to collect some from the bag. She was shocked by what she saw and said, *"Oh my God! What is it?"* asked Mr. Bankoloh, but she didn't respond to his question. She was standing there wordless, so Mr. Bankoloh went there to see what was really going on. To his surprise, instead of rice, he saw sand in the bag. When he saw the reality, he collapsed fainted and was in coma for complete one month. While he was in coma, his wife tried very hard, but she was unable to successfully sustain her children while taking care of her husband. During that period, she lost two of her firstborn children.

It was later that Mrs. Bankoloh came to understand the real story of their journey.

The day Mrs. Bankoloh knew the truth about her husband's journey with his friend; it was the very day Mr. Bankoloh started getting better.

The day she understood the whole story, she said to herself: *"I said it! I never expected such a wicked plan from my husband towards his friend. Anyway, I will go visit them and start to ask for forgiveness on their behalf."* She went to Mr. Yikiban and started begging and explaining their present situation.

Mr. Yikiban wanted to deny her apology, but his wife joined Mrs. Bankoloh to beg him. He finally agreed, but on one condition. He said Mr. Bankoloh should be the one to break the barrier he built so that he can realize his mistakes and learn a lesson. Mr. Yikiban gave her some rice and said, *"This is only for you and your children. If he accepts and realizes his mistakes, I will forgive him because the Bible advises us to forgive one another."* After all, Mrs. Bankoloh got back home to take care of her family.

When she got home, her husband asked her where she was coming from. She replied to him by saying, *"From the pit you dug, trying to fill it."* He understood straight away that she was from Mr. Yikiban's place. She explained everything to him, telling him that he is the only person that can break the barrier he created. After hearing from his wife, showing him the rice

Mr. Yikiban gave to them, he accepted to go and apologize to Mr. Yikiban.

They started living happily again, though they had lost two (2) of their four (4) children because of her husband's greed and selfishness. After two weeks, he was strong enough to walk and also talk clearly. He regretted his behavior towards his friend and he was ready to end the war between him and his friend. He asked his wife to accompany him to Mr. Yikiban's residence in order for him to say sorry to him.

Mr. Bankoloh and his wife went to Mr. Yikiban's place, and they were warmly welcomed, observing all their greeting and welcoming rites. After all that, Mr. Bankoloh started crying and begging his friend to forgive him for God's sake. Mr. Yikiban accepted his apology, though at his first attempt to beg, he rejected him.

They all condemned Mr. Bankoloh's actions towards his friend, saying *"if you want to cure a sore, you have to clean it first; then the medicine can be added later."* Following Mr. Yikiban's acceptance, they started singing and dancing to their cultural songs joyously. At the end of the reunion, they all came together and shouted, *"Let us forget about the past, at least we are happy and united again."*

They were all happy and lived as mutual friends again.

EXERCISE PAGES